SCELIDOSAURUS
(ske-LI-doh-SAW-rus)

TYRANNOSAURUS
(tie-RAN-oh-SAW-rus)

TRICERATOPS
(try-SER-a-tops)

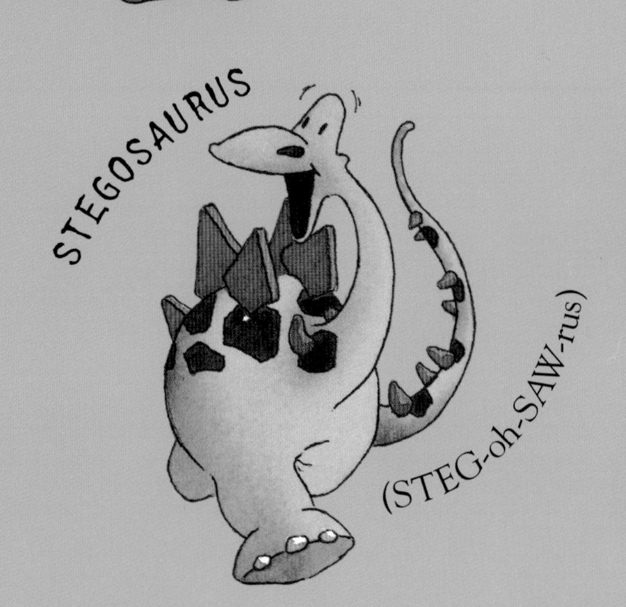
STEGOSAURUS
(STEG-oh-SAW-rus)

APATOSAURUS
(a-PAT-oh-SAW-rus)

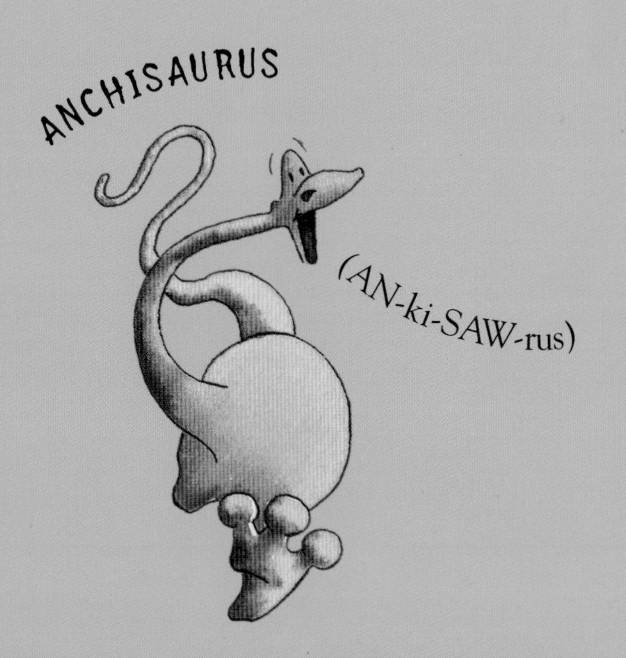
ANCHISAURUS
(AN-ki-SAW-rus)

For Frank Ritter, who's a big Harry fan—*I.W.*

For Rhian—*A.R.*

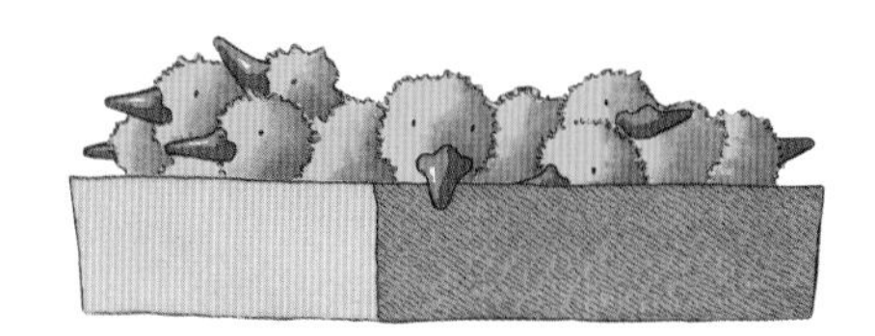

Published in the United States by Random House Children's Books, a division of Random House, Inc., New York. First published in 2003 by Puffin Books, a division of the Penguin Group, 80 Strand, London WC2R 0RL, England.

www.randomhouse.com/kids

Library of Congress Cataloging-in-Publication Data
Whybrow, Ian. Harry and the dinosaurs make a Christmas wish / by Ian Whybrow ;
illustrated by Adrian Reynolds. — 1st American ed.
p. cm.
SUMMARY: When Harry brings his toy dinosaurs to Mr. Oakley's farm, they all decide they want a duckling, and even though Mr. Oakley says they only have room at their house for chickens, they wish very hard and ask Santa to deliver a duckling.
ISBN 0-375-83111-8
[1. Wishes—Fiction. 2. Dinosaurs—Fiction. 3. Toys—Fiction.
4. Ducks—Fiction. 5. Christmas—Fiction.] I. Reynolds, Adrian, ill. II. Title.
PZ7.W6225Hao 2004
[E]—dc2 2004001361

MANUFACTURED IN CHINA First American Edition 10 9 8 7 6 5 4 3 2 1

Harry and the Dinosaurs make a Christmas Wish

Ian Whybrow and Adrian Reynolds

Random House New York

It was always fun to visit Mr. Oakley's farm. One time, he had some ducklings keeping warm in a box by the stove.

Harry took the bucketful of dinosaurs to see.

Mr. Oakley showed them one little duckling just coming out of its shell.

Harry even held the duckling in his hands.

"Raaah! Ask him, Harry!" said the dinosaurs. "Ask Mr. Oakley for a duckling to keep."

Mr. Oakley said better not. They only had room for chickens over at Harry's house.

Mr. Oakley let Harry and the dinosaurs ride home in his trailer, but they were still upset.

"Shame," said Triceratops.

"Raaah!" said Tyrannosaurus. "We want a duckling!"

"Oh, I wish we could have one!" said Harry.

It was a big wish, but it didn't work.

Maybe it was the wrong time for wishing.

At last, one cold day in the winter, the right time came.

Gran said, “Harry, will you and the dinosaurs help me stir up the Christmas cookie batter?”

They all had a good stir and a lick—
and then they closed their eyes and they
made a special wish, a *Christmas* wish!

Harry wrote down his wish in a letter to Santa.
"What did you wish for?" asked Mom.
"A duckling!" said Harry and the dinosaurs.

"Well . . . let's look in the shops before you send that letter," said Mom. "Just in case you change your mind."

"Good idea!" said Gran. "I want to spend my savings out of my egg-shaped piggy bank!"

They all went on the bus to see the lights and the Christmas displays in the big stores.

Harry found just the right book about dinosaurs in the bookshop.

And there was plenty Harry liked in the toy shop!
So he thought of lots more things to put in his letter.

"But don't forget to ask for our duckling, Harry," whispered the dinosaurs.

On Christmas Eve, Gran helped Harry to hang up his stocking.

"Dinosaurs don't like presents in stockings," said Harry. "They want their present in an egg."

"I see," said Gran. "Then we'll leave out my piggy bank, shall we?"

Sam said it was stupid putting out an egg. Eggs were for Easter, not for Christmas.

That was why Harry and the dinosaurs made *Raaah* noises all through her favorite TV show.

Gran took Harry to his room to settle down.

"I've been bad to Sam, haven't I?" sighed Harry. "Now I won't get my Christmas wishes."

Gran said not to get upset. Christmas wishes were special, and if you were really sorry, Santa would understand.

When Harry opened his eyes, it was Christmas morning!

"Wake up, my Apatosaurus, my Anchisaurus, and my Triceratops!" called Harry.

And he called, "Wake up!" to his Stegosaurus and his Scelidosaurus and his Tyrannosaurus and all the sleepy old dinosaurs.

They jumped up and rushed downstairs to see what Santa had left for them.

Harry unwrapped all his presents.

"Just what I wanted!" he shouted every time.

"What a shame," sighed the dinosaurs. "Santa didn't bring us a duckling."

"Wait!" said Harry. "You haven't opened your egg yet!"

So all the dinosaurs closed their eyes, gave the egg a warm rub, and made a Christmas wish.

And guess what popped out . . .

. . . a baby Pterodactyl!

"Raah! Much better than a duckling!" said Scelidosaurus.
"Raaah! It's a flying dinosaur!" said Tyrannosaurus.
"Raaaaaah to you, too," said Pterodactyl.
Merry Ch-*RAAAAAAH*-stmas, Harry!

SCELIDOSAURUS

(ske-LI-doh-SAW-rus)

TYRANNOSAURUS

(tie-RAN-oh-SAW-rus)

TRICERATOPS

(try-SER-a-tops)

STEGOSAURUS

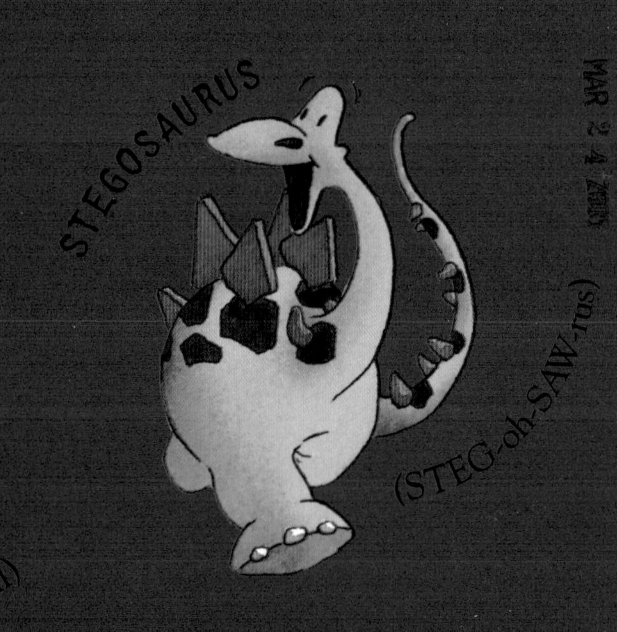

(STEG-oh-SAW-rus)

PTERODACTYL

(TER-oh-DAC-til)

APATOSAURUS

(a-PAT-oh-SAW-rus)

ANCHISAURUS

(AN-ki-SAW-rus)